DATE DUE	
MR 14 '01		
AP 18 '01	SE 1 3 '07	
OC 11 '01		
JV 01 '02	AP 27 '09	
JY 03 '03	JE 2 4 '09	
OC 1 3 '04		
FE 3 '05		
JE 24 '06		
JY 06 '06		
JY 2 0 '07		
AG 1 1 '07		
AG 2 3 '07		

F
J   Murphy, Elspeth C.
           The mystery of the painted
           snake

           Three cousins detective club
           #29

THREE COUSINS DETECTIVE CLUB®

The Mystery of the Painted Snake

Elspeth Campbell Murphy

Illustrated by Joe Nordstrom

BETHANY HOUSE PUBLISHERS
MINNEAPOLIS, MINNESOTA 55438

Published by Bethany House Publishers
A Ministry of Bethany Fellowship International
11400 Hampshire Avenue South
Bloomington, Minnesota 55438
www.bethanyhouse.com

Printed in the United States of America by
Bethany Press International, Bloomington, Minnesota 55438

Library of Congress Cataloging-in-Publication Data

Murphy, Elspeth Campbell.
    The mystery of the painted snake / by Elspeth Campbell Murphy ;
illustrated by Joe Nordstrom.
        p.   cm. — (Three Cousins Detective Club ; 29)
Summary: After Timothy copies a papier-mâché snake from a mural
for a Christmas present for Titus, he and his cousins find that the
snake on the mural has changed.
    ISBN 0–7642–2137–X (pbk.)
    [1. Painting—Fiction. 2. Cousins—Fiction. 3. Mystery and
detective stories.] I. Nordstrom, Joe, ill. II. Title.
    PZ7.M95316 Myee   2000
    [Fic]—dc21

                  00–010528

ELSPETH CAMPBELL MURPHY has been a familiar name in Christian publishing for over twenty years, with more than one hundred books to her credit and sales approaching six million worldwide. She is the author of the bestselling series *David and I Talk to God* and *The Kids From Apple Street Church,* as well as the 1990 Gold Medallion winner *Do You See Me, God?,* and two books of prayer meditations for teachers, *Chalkdust* and *Recess.* A graduate of Trinity College and Moody Bible Institute, Elspeth and her husband, Mike, make their home in Chicago, where she writes full time.

Contents

Write these things for the future.
Then people who are not yet born
will praise the Lord.

Psalm 102:18

1

Papier-Mâché

*C*hristmas came early to Timothy Dawson's house.

That's not how Timothy planned it.

But there was nothing like a baby sister to mess up a person's plans.

It happened when Priscilla found a Christmas present that Timothy had so *carefully* hidden.

The present wasn't for her. But that didn't matter to Priscilla.

Keeping Priscilla out of his stuff was always a big problem for Timothy. But lately it had become a HUMONGOUS problem.

That was because Timothy, who was very good at art, had really gotten into papier-mâché.

He had learned how to make wonderful things out of paper and paste in a special class at the Community Arts Center. Everyone was getting something made of papier-mâché from Timothy for Christmas this year. Including his cousins Sarah-Jane Cooper and Titus McKay.

The problem was, Priscilla positively *adored* all the brightly painted wonderful things Timothy was making.

Nothing was safe from her busy little hands.

Timothy's father had put a hook latch high on the outside of the door for when Timothy was gone from his room.

So far the latch was working pretty well. But Timothy knew it was only a matter of time before Priscilla figured out how to climb up on something and unhook it.

There was a latch on the inside of the door, too, for when Timothy was in his room.

He was there now, playing a game with his visiting cousins, Titus and Sarah-Jane, when the doorknob turned. The door opened a little way before it was caught by the latch.

"Saywah-Zane?" said a pleading little voice from the other side of the door.

Timothy and Titus groaned.

Priscilla knew perfectly well that when she wanted to break into the big kids, the weakest link was Sarah-Jane.

Sarah-Jane simply couldn't resist little kids.

Especially not Priscilla.

"Saywah-Zane?"

Sarah-Jane looked helplessly at the boys.

"Oh, go ahead," sighed Timothy. "If we don't let her in, she'll just stand out there and cry."

Sarah-Jane went to open the door.

"Hi, Saywah-Zane."

"Hi, Pris—"

Suddenly, Sarah-Jane jumped back and screamed.

2

Toddler Trouble

*E*ven before he saw what Priscilla was holding, Timothy knew the awful truth.

He knew by the way Sarah-Jane scrambled up to the top bunk.

That was because Sarah-Jane positively hated snakes.

And Priscilla was holding a snake by the tail.

It was a long, thin snake.

Bright light green.

With black spots and lines all along its back.

It wasn't real.

It was made of papier-mâché.

But it certainly *looked* real.

"EX-cellent snake!" exclaimed Titus, as if he couldn't believe his eyes.

Titus positively loved snakes. He loved all

kinds of animals. But his mother had a "thing" about snakes just like Sarah-Jane did. So his parents always said no whenever the subject of getting a pet snake happened to come up.

"I'm glad you like it, Ti," Timothy said, "because it's your Christmas present from me. I figured a papier-mâché snake was the next best thing to a real one." He glared at Priscilla. "It was *supposed* to be a *surprise.*"

"Pwitty 'nake," said Priscilla happily.

"Mine?" gasped Titus, as if he couldn't believe his ears. The very idea was so exciting that he screamed. And Titus never screamed.

"OK, Sib," Timothy said to Priscilla. "Give the snake to Titus. It's his Christmas present, after all."

Priscilla shook her head wildly back and forth. "NO! NO! NO! MINE! MINE! MINE!"

"It's Ti's snake," said Timothy firmly.

Titus sauntered over and casually tried to take the snake away from her. But that only made Priscilla clutch the snake tighter. She ran into a corner, screaming.

And when it came to screaming, Priscilla could make more noise than Sarah-Jane and Titus put together.

"What on earth is going on in there?" called Timothy's mother.

"Nothing," Timothy called back. "Everything's OK. I know what to do."

His cousins and his sister watched in surprise as Timothy flopped on his stomach on the floor. He crawled so far under the bed that only his sneakers showed. When he crawled back out he was holding a papier-mâché pig.

He held the pig out to Priscilla.

Priscilla *loved* pigs.

She dropped the snake and grabbed the pig.

Fast as lightning, Titus snatched up the snake and put it on the top shelf of the bookcase.

Priscilla barely noticed. "Piggy!" she squealed, sounding like a little piglet herself. "Pwitty piggy!"

"Merry Christmas," said Timothy. "But don't come crying to me when you have one less present to open on Christmas morning."

"Pwitty piggy," said Priscilla. "Mine piggy. Show Mommy."

"Good idea!" said Timothy. "Show Mommy."

Priscilla toddled happily out of the room, and Timothy collapsed on the floor.

For such a cute little thing, Priscilla really was exhausting.

3

Detectives

"Just out of curiosity," said Titus. "Where did you hide the snake?"

"In the upstairs hall closet," said Timothy. "Inside a big roll of wrapping paper."

Titus and Sarah-Jane nodded thoughtfully.

Timothy could tell they were impressed.

He had thought it was a great hiding place, too. Until it had been raided by a baby.

Sarah-Jane seemed to guess what Timothy was thinking. "Priscilla couldn't have found it *on purpose*," she said. "It must have been *by accident*. Or maybe she *saw* you hide the snake."

This cheered Timothy up a bit.

The three cousins had a detective club, and they took pride in their work. As detectives, they were all very good at hiding things.

"It was a good spot," agreed Titus. "But . . . um . . . I couldn't help noticing that you didn't hide it in the room here."

"Ha!" said Timothy.

That was because when Titus visited, he stayed in Timothy's room.

And the cousins were all very good at *finding* things, too.

"I'm not a snoop," said Titus innocently.

"No, of course not!" said Timothy. "The thought never entered my mind. But you might have found it *accidentally.*"

Sarah-Jane didn't say anything. From her perch on the top bunk, she just looked around the room.

Super casually.

Timothy knew she was too polite to come right out and say, "Where's my present?" But it wasn't too hard to tell that's what she was thinking.

"Oh, all right, S-J. You can have your Christmas present now, too."

"It's not a snake, is it?" asked Sarah-Jane.

"No," said Timothy. "It's not a snake."

4

Sid

*T*imothy had to reach an out-of-the-way spot. So he dragged a chair over to the bookcase.

He handed the snake to Titus. Then he reached down behind a row of books on the top shelf and pulled out a papier-mâché bracelet.

It was blue, painted all over with beautiful angels.

Timothy had figured angels were good for a Christmas present because of the angels that appeared to the shepherds when Jesus was born. But he also figured Sarah-Jane could wear the bracelet all year long, too. Angels were good to have around anytime.

Sarah-Jane screamed when she saw her present. (This time it was a happy scream, not a scared one!) Sarah-Jane was so happy with her present that she could even be nice about Titus's.

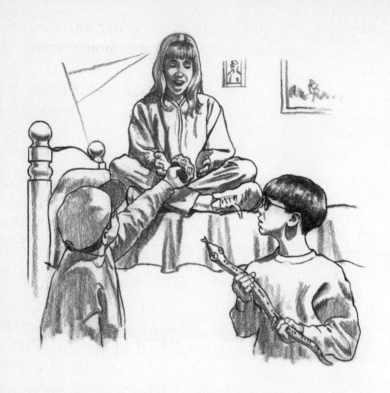

She looked down on it from where she was still perched on the top bunk and said, "You know, that really is a beautiful snake. I love the color."

"It's the same color as a green tree python," said Titus happily.

"That's what Sid started out as," said Timothy.

"Sid?" asked Titus.

"That's what I called him," said Timothy.

"But you can change his name if you like."

"No, no," said Titus. "Sid is good. I like Sid."

Now that she knew the snake had a name, Sarah-Jane seemed to think it was safe to come down.

She even seemed to feel it was safe to pick him up. Carefully.

"I love the design on his back," she said.

Titus nodded. "Green tree pythons don't have designs on their backs. But I like the way this looks. I like the spots and lines a lot."

"Glad to hear it," said Timothy. "Because it was kind of funny the way that worked out."

"Funny ha-ha? Or funny weird?" asked Titus, stroking Sid's head as if he were a real pet.

"Funny weird," said Timothy. "Definitely funny weird."

Titus and Sarah-Jane looked at him in surprise.

What could be funny-weird about the design on a papier-mâché snake?

5

Spots and Lines

"Well, see," began Timothy, "I got the idea from the Arts Center. "We had this visiting artist, Mr. Bell."

"Is he the one who taught you to make papier-mâché?" asked Sarah-Jane, turning her bracelet around on her wrist.

"No, that was the director, Mrs. Martin. She teaches classes sometimes, too. I had a still life class from Mr. Bell."

"What's a 'still life'?" asked Titus.

"It's a painting of objects," explained Timothy. "You know, like a bowl of fruit or something. Except Mr. Bell always said *anything* could be interesting to paint if we just look closely and think about it.

"We have this props closet full of all kinds of stuff. We get to take the stuff out and spread it out on the tables and play with things. Really *look* at them before we arrange them and start to paint."

Timothy sighed. "I really liked Mr. Bell. But we knew he wasn't going to be there forever.

"Anyway, before his visit was over, Mr. Bell drew the outline of an animal mural on the outside wall. And we kids got to paint it in."

Actually, Timothy was the only younger kid who got to work on the mural—all the other kids were teenagers. But he didn't want to brag about that.

Timothy went on. "The mural shows all these different animals together. I worked on the tiger. But I remembered that the snake was this really pretty green. The girl who painted it was *really* proud of it.

"Anyway, I didn't know if it was a real kind of snake or just a fantasy kind. So I looked it up in the encyclopedia. And it turns out it was a . . ."

"Green tree python," said Titus.

"Exactly," said Timothy. "A green tree python. They have a few white specks here and there. But basically they're just plain green. So that's how I made it."

"What's weird about that?" asked Sarah-Jane.

"Nothing," said Timothy. "But then one day I was over at the Arts Center. And I went to look at the mural again." (Mr. Bell had told them they would keep coming back to see their work.)

"Anyway," said Timothy. "I discovered that the snake wasn't plain at all! It had spots and lines all along its back! And I didn't even notice them before!"

As detectives, Timothy and his cousins had taught themselves to notice things. But Timothy was an artist as well as a detective. He expected himself to *doubly* notice things.

"Hey, don't worry about it," said Titus. "I really like the design."

"Well," admitted Timothy. "I do, too. I copied it down exactly on a piece of paper. Then when I got home, I looked up snakes again in the encyclopedia. I didn't see any snakes that had that design. But I liked it. So I painted it on Sid anyway. I hope that's OK."

"It's more than OK," said Titus. "It's perfect."

"Would you like to see the mural?" asked Timothy shyly. "It is pretty good, if I do say so myself."

His cousins thought this was a great idea.

And Timothy could tell they weren't just saying that to be polite.

Titus considered taking his snake. But then he decided that carrying a snake around with him might look a little odd. Because, even with the spots and lines, Sid was so realistic-looking, he might scare the neighbors.

So Titus stood on tiptoe and pushed Sid back onto the high shelf.

The next step was getting out of the house.

Priscilla was going out later to another toddler's house to play. But if she saw her brother and cousins leaving without her, there would be some serious crying.

Fortunately, as detectives, the cousins had taught themselves to move quickly and quietly.

Somehow they were able to tell Timothy's mother where they were going and get their coats on without being spotted by you-know-who.

Still, Timothy couldn't shake the feeling that in all their hurry, there was something they had forgotten to do.

6

Church Bells

*T*hey set off for the Arts Center. But they hadn't gone far when they heard bells.

"Must be a wedding or something," said Timothy. "The church on the corner rings the bells for special occasions."

"Oooh! A wedding!" cried Sarah-Jane. She took off running. The boys knew she was hoping to catch a glimpse of the bride and groom. By the time they caught up to her, Sarah-Jane had scooted toward the front of the crowd.

Someone was handing out little packets of birdseed, and Sarah-Jane took one.

"You toss the seeds at the bride and groom for good luck," she explained, unwrapping her packet. "It's better than rice, because it doesn't make a mess and later the birds can eat it. Isn't that a good idea?"

"*S-J!*" hissed Timothy. "What are you

doing?! You don't even *know* these people!"

But at that moment, the bride and groom came out of the church and ran down the walk to the car. Sarah-Jane happily cheered with everyone else and tossed her birdseed.

Timothy and Titus practically had to haul her away before she went off to the reception.

Sarah-Jane was not too happy about being hauled away.

To get her mind off it, Titus said quickly, "I heard this really good story about church bells. Do you want to hear it?"

"Oh, all right," said Sarah-Jane. Whenever she heard the word *story*, her ears perked up. And her cousins knew this about her.

"It was in the newspaper," continued Titus. "These people in England were at church for a meeting. And they accidentally got locked in. And they couldn't get to the phone. So they rang an SOS on the church bells until someone came and let them out."

"They used Morse code?" said Sarah-Jane. "Cool!"

The cousins knew about Morse code because it was written down in their matching code books. They had several different codes there so that they could send one another secret messages.

Morse code wasn't exactly a *secret* code. It used to be used by anyone to send messages by telegraph or across the water by flashing lights. But the code wasn't used much anymore, because messages could be sent by satellite. Hardly anyone had the code memorized these days. Not even the cousins.

"I guess a lot of people still know how to send an SOS for help," said Sarah-Jane.

"We do," said Timothy. "Right? The code for *S* is three short sounds. Dit-dit-dit. And the code for *O* is three long sounds. Dah-dah-dah.

And then you do dit-dit-dit again."

"Right," said Titus. "Or if you didn't have a bell, you could use a flashlight or something. Three short flashes. Three long flashes. Three short flashes."

The cousins had been so busy talking about Morse code that they had arrived at the Arts Center almost before they knew it.

"The mural is right over here," said Timothy. "It's pretty neat-O, if I do say so myself."

"EX-cellent!" agreed Titus.

"So cool!" agreed Sarah-Jane.

They went closer to get a better look.

"And there's the snake I was telling you about. . . ."

Timothy stopped dead in his tracks and stared. He opened his mouth, but no more sound came out.

That's because the snake in the mural was plain green.

There wasn't a spot or a line on it.

7

The Snake in the Mural

"OK," declared Timothy. "I am *not* crazy!"

"No one ever said you were," said Titus soothingly—as if he were talking to somebody totally nuts.

"I am not crazy," repeated Timothy.

"Of course not!" said Sarah-Jane.

"There was a *design* on that snake," said Timothy.

Sarah-Jane and Titus glanced at each other with raised eyebrows.

"There was!" cried Timothy. "How else would I have gotten the idea to put it on Sid? I didn't just make up that design! I copied it off the snake in the mural. I did."

Titus thought about this for a moment. "OK, that makes sense. But then, where did the design go? It's not there now."

"Look!" cried Sarah-Jane suddenly, pointing at the ground.

There were drops of something on the grass. Something bright light green. Something much brighter and lighter than the green of the grass, which was a dull, brownish green.

Instead, the green drops on the ground exactly matched the green of the snake.

"Paint?" said Timothy. *"Paint?"*

He leaned closer and looked intently at the snake.

"Look!" he cried. "Look! Look! You can see the design! Just a little bit, showing through. I'm *not* crazy. There *was* a design on that snake! And . . . and somebody covered it up!"

Titus and Sarah-Jane looked closely and agreed that Timothy was right.

"We never *really* thought you were crazy before, Tim," said Sarah-Jane.

"Of course not," agreed Titus. "But it's just nice to have proof."

"OK. So we agree I'm not crazy now," said Timothy. "And you know what? I don't think I was crazy before, either. I think the reason I didn't notice a design on the snake at first was because—*the design wasn't there!*"

Titus said slowly, "Earlier you said that the girl who painted the snake was really proud of it. . . ."

Timothy saw what Titus was getting at. He nodded excitedly. "Carolyn. I don't know her last name. But I know where she lives, because I had to drop some stuff off at her house one time."

The cousins looked at one another.

It couldn't hurt to drop in on Carolyn and ask her a few questions.

8

The T.C.D.C.

*T*he cousins were in luck.

They found Carolyn at home, and she remembered Timothy.

"What can I do for you?" she asked. She seemed a little surprised to find three "little kids" on her doorstep, but she sounded friendly enough.

"We wanted to ask you about the snake you painted on the mural at the Arts Center," said Timothy.

Instantly, Carolyn stiffened. "What about it?" she asked.

The cousins glanced at one another. Was it their imagination—or did Carolyn suddenly sound nervous?

"It's a green tree python," said Titus.

"Yeah. So?"

"So green tree pythons don't have marks on

their backs," said Sarah-Jane carefully. "But this one did—for a while, anyway. And we just wondered if you knew anything about that."

"What makes you think *I* know anything?" asked Carolyn.

Timothy sighed. This was slow going.

Sarah-Jane tried again. "We just wondered what happened to the design. Did you try it out and then decide that you liked the snake better plain? Artists do that when they're making things, don't they? Change their minds, I mean?"

"Me!" exclaimed Carolyn indignantly. *"I* didn't put that silly design on the snake!"

"Then you do know about the design," said Timothy.

"Of course I know about it! I'm the one who . . ." She stopped and sighed. "OK, look. I snuck some paint home, OK? It was left over from doing the snake on the mural. And it was such a pretty color, I thought I could use it for something at home. But then one day I just happened to be over by the mural."

Checking out your work, Timothy thought.

"Go on," he said.

"And I couldn't believe it!" cried Carolyn. "Someone had scribbled graffiti all over my snake. My beautiful, beautiful snake! It's supposed to be just plain."

"Because it's a green tree python," said Titus.

"Exactly!" said Carolyn. "So I came home and got my leftover paint and covered over the markings."

"And you didn't tell Mrs. Martin or anybody at the Center about it?" asked Timothy.

Carolyn looked a little embarrassed. "No, I didn't. I should have, I guess. I wasn't thinking. I was just so mad about someone messing with my work."

Timothy nodded and muttered to himself, "And you don't even have a baby sister, do you?"

"What?" asked Carolyn.

"Nothing," said Timothy. "Thanks for clearing up the mystery for the T.C.D.C."

"What's a 'teesy-deesy'?" asked Carolyn.

"It's letters," explained Sarah-Jane. "Capital T. Capital C. Capital D. Capital C. It stands for the Three Cousins Detective Club."

"Detectives, huh?" said Carolyn. "Well, if you really want to solve a mystery, find out what kind of nut goes around scribbling graffiti on other people's snakes!"

"Hmm," said Titus thoughtfully when

Carolyn had gone inside and firmly shut the door.

"What?" asked Timothy and Sarah-Jane together.

"It's just . . . those markings you copied onto Sid . . ." said Titus.

"What about them?" asked Timothy.

Titus shrugged. "They don't look like graffiti to me."

9

Dots and Dashes

*T*imothy and Sarah-Jane looked at Titus with interest.

He tried to explain. "See—graffiti is usually there to mess things up. Or else it's there to get attention. Do you know what I mean? If some kids had wanted to mess up the mural, they would have spray-painted the whole thing. Or if they had wanted to do their own mural some-where, they would still have used great big let-ters and bright colors."

"Right," said Sarah-Jane. "And Sid's mark-ings were small and delicate. You would really have to look closely to notice them. They couldn't have been made with spray paint. Someone used a little paintbrush to make all those spots and lines."

Timothy didn't say anything. He was trying to picture just how the design looked.

There was something odd about it.

The way it had a few marks.

Then a space.

Then a few more marks.

Then a space . . .

Suddenly, a little lightbulb lit up in Timothy's head.

"Not spots and lines," he whispered. "Dots and dashes!"

Without another word, the cousins turned and ran all the way back home.

When they got there, they found a note from Timothy's mother, telling them she had left lunch for them in the fridge.

But they couldn't stop to think about that.

They had to take another look at Sid.

NOW.

There was just one problem.

When they burst into Timothy's room, Sid was gone.

10

The Search for Sid

*I*n a flash, Timothy realized what he had forgotten to do when they left home.

Latch the door to his room.

"And look," he said. "We conveniently left the chair under the bookcase for her. All she had to do was climb up and grab Sid."

"You don't know for sure it was Priscilla," Sarah-Jane protested. Sometimes she figured girl cousins had to stick together.

"Right," said Titus. "It was those pesky elves."

"OK, OK," said Sarah-Jane. "Let's just figure out where she put him."

They did a quick but thorough search of Timothy's room.

No Sid.

Titus said, "We could call her up at her little friend's house and just ask her where she

41

put him." He didn't sound as if he thought this was the best idea he'd ever had.

"Have you ever tried to get a straight answer out of that kid?" asked Timothy.

Nevertheless, it was worth a try. He told Titus and Sarah-Jane to keep looking upstairs while he called Priscilla.

"Hopeless," said Timothy when he returned. "Absolutely hopeless. She just kept saying, 'OK. Bye.' "

"Aha!" cried Sarah-Jane as a sudden thought struck her. "Maybe Priscilla put Sid back where she found him. Maybe she thought that's where he belonged. And she was just being a good little helper."

Timothy wasn't sure about the good-little-helper part. But he agreed that it was a great idea to look in the roll of wrapping paper in the upstairs hall closet.

There was only one problem. Sid wasn't there.

"This is humiliating," Timothy muttered. "Priscilla found my hiding place, but I can't find hers!"

"I'm hungry," sighed Sarah-Jane as they went downstairs. "You guys keep looking. I'll set out the lunch stuff and call you when it's ready."

Timothy and Titus heard Sarah-Jane go into the kitchen and open the refrigerator.

This was followed by an ear-shattering scream.

"I think she found Sid," said Titus.

11

Morse Code

"What on *earth* was she *thinking*?" gasped Sarah-Jane, clasping her hand over her chest.

She had sort of gotten over her first fear of Sid. Now she had to get over the shock of finding him in the refrigerator.

Timothy smacked his forehead. "Why didn't I think of looking there before? It's Priscilla's favorite place to put things. You know, like the TV remote. The car keys. It's usually the first place we look when something's missing."

The cousins thought about this for a moment, but it seemed there was nothing they could say.

Suddenly, they remembered why they were there.

Sid.

They had to know if the peculiar marks

meant anything or not. Timothy's idea was that the spots and lines were really dots and dashes. In other words, a message in Morse code.

There was only one way to find out.

Timothy went to get his code book while Titus and Sarah-Jane set out lunch.

Timothy opened his book to the page for Morse code, which looked like this:

A	•–	J	•–––	S	•••
B	–•••	K	–•–	T	–
C	–•–•	L	•–••	U	••–
D	–••	M	––	V	•••–
E	•	N	–•	W	•––
F	••–•	O	–––	X	–••–
G	––•	P	•––•	Y	–•––
H	••••	Q	––•–	Z	––••
I	••	R	•–•		

Then the three detective cousins sat around the kitchen table, munching sandwiches and trying to read a papier-mâché snake.

The markings started at the back of Sid's head and went all the way down to his tail. There were little spaces between some groups of markings, with some bigger spaces along the way.

Timothy said, "If we're right about this, the little spaces might separate the letters. And the bigger spaces might separate the words."

The marks along Sid's back looked like this:

•• —• — •••• • •—• • —•• •••• •— —

The cousins decided that Titus would read off the dots and dashes.

Timothy would look them up on the chart in the code book.

And Sarah-Jane would write the letters on a piece of paper.

"OK," said Titus. "Here we go. The first two marks are Dot Dot. Does that stand for anything?"

"Yes!" cried Timothy. "Yes! Dot Dot stands for the letter *I*!"

Timothy, Titus, and Sarah-Jane looked at one another in excitement. Up until now the idea of a secret message had been just that—an idea. Now they knew they were really on to something.

As fast as they possibly could, they decoded the message. Letter by letter. Word by word.

When they were done, Sarah-Jane sat back and looked at the message she had neatly printed on the paper. She said, "*That* can't be right. *Can* it?"

12

The Secret Message

*T*hey tried again.

This time Sarah-Jane read off the dots and dashes. Titus looked them up on the chart. And Timothy wrote down the letters on the paper.

The message came out the same.

In the red hat.

Titus stared down at Sid in disbelief. "That's it?" he asked. "My beautiful snake says, 'In the red hat'?"

"I'm really sorry," said Timothy. "I can paint over it for you if you want me to."

"No, no," said Titus quickly. "Sid is even more interesting this way with his weird message. I like weird." He paused. "But why would someone go to all the trouble of painting a weird message like that on the mural?"

Sarah-Jane said slowly, "I know what the

words *mean*. But what do they *mean*?"

Titus said, "What do you mean, 'what do they mean?' "

Sarah-Jane said excitedly, "Maybe it's a top secret code. Like when one spy says to the other one, 'The owl flies at midnight.' Only he's not really talking about owls. He's talking about the stolen plans. They're being smuggled out of the country tonight!"

Sarah-Jane read a lot, and she had a vivid imagination.

Timothy looked at her, thoroughly confused. "What stolen plans?"

Titus heaved an exasperated sigh. "Honestly, S-J! I don't know anything about owls or stolen plans. I just think the message means there's something in a red hat. Period."

"Stolen plans," suggested Sarah-Jane.

"Aurggh!" replied Titus.

"Abraham Lincoln used to carry letters around in his hat," said Sarah-Jane.

"Yes, but that was a top hat," said Titus, who had once played Abraham Lincoln in a school play.

"So?" said Sarah-Jane. "A hat's a hat."

"*What* hat?" cried Timothy. "What *hat*?"

This was maybe not the most meaningful conversation the three of them had ever had.

They stopped to take a deep breath.

"OK," said Titus super calmly. "Someone painted a weird message on the snake in the mural. But we don't know why or what the message means."

"Or who it was for," said Sarah-Jane.

The boys looked at her in surprise. This was a new idea.

"*Somebody* was supposed to read it, right?" said Sarah-Jane. "Somebody who would know what it meant."

"And we don't even know if that person got the message," said Timothy.

Now Titus and Sarah-Jane looked at him in surprise.

"Think about it," said Timothy. "Carolyn painted over the message. . . ."

"Because she thought it was graffiti," added Sarah-Jane.

"So maybe Tim is the only one who saw the marks on the snake and realized it was a hidden message," said Titus. He looked down at Sid again. "And now we have the only copy."

13

Questions

Plenty of questions.

And no answers.

But there was one thing the cousins *did* know for certain: They couldn't just sit around doing nothing.

Timothy said, "The hidden message was on the mural at the Arts Center. So maybe somebody at the Arts Center knows what it means. It wouldn't hurt to go back and ask."

Titus and Sarah-Jane agreed that this was a great idea.

Or at least a good idea.

Or at least it was a place to start.

They quickly cleared up their lunch stuff and got their coats.

This time Titus had no intention of leaving Sid alone and helpless with Priscilla.

And speaking of Priscilla—the cousins

realized she would probably be back any minute. They had to make a break for it before she came home and caught them going somewhere without her.

Too late.

They were just headed out the door as Priscilla and her mother were coming in.

Quickly, Titus zipped Sid inside his jacket so that only his head was peeking out. It looked a little odd. But what were you going to do?

"Pwitty 'nake," said Priscilla.

"Forget about it," said Titus.

"Where going?" asked Priscilla.

"Out," said Timothy.

"Sibby go?" said Priscilla.

It was not a question that had a good answer.

If they said no, the crying would break your heart—and your eardrums.

If they said yes, they'd be taking a baby along on an investigation.

"I'll take charge of her," Sarah-Jane murmured.

Timothy sighed. "OK, Sib. Get your stroller. But we've got important stuff to do. So just don't embarrass me, OK?"

"OK," said Priscilla happily.

Famous last words.

14

Toys!

One thing worried the cousins as they walked back to the Arts Center. And that was how to tell Mrs. Martin about the snake without getting Carolyn in trouble.

But, as it turned out, they didn't have to worry about that.

Carolyn was already there, talking to Mrs. Martin about the graffiti on the snake and how she had painted over it.

They both looked up and smiled at the cousins as they came in. So things seemed to be going all right.

Priscilla demanded to get out of her stroller. There didn't seem to be anything sitting out that she could wreck. So Timothy figured it would be all right to let her toddle around the room.

"It wasn't graffiti," Carolyn said to the

cousins, sounding more than a little embarrassed.

It wouldn't have been nice to say, "Tell me something I don't know," so Timothy didn't say anything.

Carolyn added, "Mrs. Martin says it was something Mr. Bell often did in his work."

Timothy could feel his mouth fall open. Carolyn had told him something he didn't know.

"*Mr. Bell* put the message on the mural?" cried Timothy.

"Yes," said Mrs. Martin. "He likes to include words, bits of poetry. Sometimes it's written out. Sometimes it's in shorthand. Sometimes it's even in Morse code."

"That's what the marks probably were," said Carolyn. "But now we'll never know what the message said."

The cousins looked at one another. Sometimes you just have to say, "TAA-DAA!"

They said it now as Titus plopped Sid down on the table.

"I copied the marks from the mural before I even knew what they were," Timothy explained. "I just thought they were pretty. But then we realized they were Morse code. And we figured out what it says. But we don't know what it means."

"What does it say?" asked Carolyn.

Mrs. Martin, who was one of those people who still knew Morse code, said, "It says 'in the red hat.' "

The cousins looked at one another again. They had figured they were right about the message. But it was nice to *know* they were right.

"But what does it *mean*?" asked Carolyn.

"That's what *we'd* like to know!" said Sarah-Jane.

"It probably doesn't mean anything," said Mrs. Martin. "Probably Mr. Bell just liked the sound of the words. Or the look of the dots and dashes."

"You mean there *is* no red hat?" asked Titus.

Mrs. Martin shrugged. "If there is, I have no idea where it is."

"Or what's in it," said Sarah-Jane.

"Or what's in it," agreed Mrs. Martin.

Timothy sighed. It was all very disappointing.

Everyone must have been thinking the same thing, because they all just sat there without saying anything. The room was very quiet.

Too quiet, Timothy suddenly realized.

A room with Priscilla in it was never quiet—unless she was sound asleep or up to something.

Timothy looked around in a panic.

Sure enough, Priscilla had gotten into the props cabinet and pulled everything out onto the floor.

"TOYS!" she said happily when Timothy went over to get her.

"They're not toys, they're props," Timothy groaned.

"PWOPS!" said Priscilla.

Timothy was so busy trying to put things away that it took him a moment to realize that Priscilla was wearing something on her head.

A red hat.

15

The Letter

"OK," said Timothy, taking a deep breath. "I am *not* crazy. There was *no red hat* in the props cabinet before! I would have *noticed* it."

"Well, it's certainly there now," said Titus.

"I've never seen it before," said Mrs. Martin.

"Me, neither," said Carolyn.

"Me, needer," said Priscilla.

"Is it *the* hat?" asked Sarah-Jane. "The one from the mural? Is there something inside it?"

"Only one way to find out," said Timothy.

But that would mean getting it away from the little person who was wearing it.

Sarah-Jane smiled brightly at Priscilla. "I love your hat, Little Sweetie Face! Can Sarah-Jane try it on?"

Priscilla appeared to be thinking this over.

"I'll let you wear my bracelet," said Sarah-

Jane. "See, Priscilla? See all the beautiful angels?"

"Wow! Cool bracelet!" exclaimed Carolyn. "Can I try it on after Priscilla, Sarah-Jane?"

"Sure," said Sarah-Jane. "Timothy made it, you know."

"You're kidding!"

"No, really. He did."

"That's fantastic," said Carolyn.

"It's a Christmas present," said Sarah-Jane. "But it's not just for wearing at Christmas."

"No," agreed Carolyn. "You can wear angels anytime."

Titus buried his head in his hands and made a very loud moaning sound. "Ladies, please. I'm begging you. Can we just please, please, please get *on* with it?"

"Mine!" said Priscilla, reaching for the bracelet so no one else could get to it first.

"Fair trade," Sarah-Jane told her firmly. "If you get to wear my bracelet, I get to wear your hat."

Sarah-Jane might have been crazy about little kids. But she was also one tough cookie when it came to trades. Without another word, Priscilla gave Sarah-Jane the hat, and everyone heaved a sigh of relief.

Then they turned the hat over and looked inside.

No one was really surprised to see big X stitches on the lining. They could feel something hidden inside.

Quickly, Mrs. Martin undid the stitches and pulled out an envelope.

Inside the envelope was a letter. It was addressed to Mrs. Martin and the staff of the Arts Center. And it was from the artist, Mr. Bell.

The letter said:

> *I can't begin to tell you what a wonderful time I've had, working at your Center as visiting artist! As you know, I've continually told the students to* notice, *really* notice *the world around them. So I placed this hat in the props cabinet to see if anyone would notice the stitches and feel the letter inside. And you did! Otherwise you wouldn't be reading this. Also, I left a clue on the mural. I knew the students would be going back to look at their painting! Please accept this gift to help you with the work you're doing training our future artists.*

At this point Mrs. Martin unfolded a check and gulped when she saw the amount.

She wouldn't tell them how much it was for, but she said the board of directors was going to be very, very happy.

"Wait," said Carolyn. "There's a P.S."

"Yes, there is," said Mrs. Martin. She read it aloud:

> *P.S.: While all of the kids were great to work with, I want you to particularly keep your eye on a young boy named Timothy Dawson. I hope we can help him to develop his God-given talent. I will look forward to seeing his work in the future.*

Timothy felt his face getting hot. And he knew without even looking in the mirror that his face was getting bright, bright pink. But at the same time he felt a wonderful shiver of pure happiness.

Titus clapped Timothy on the back.

Then he looked around and said, "Hey, where's Sid? I'd better hold on to him. He might be worth big bucks someday."

But Sid was not on the table where they'd left him.

"Oooo!" said a little voice from under the table. "Pwitty 'nake. Mine! Mine!"

The End